A STEPPING STONE BOOK™

Random House 🏠 New York

Library of Congress Control Number: 2005931710

ISBN-13: 978-0-7364-2346-5
ISBN-10: 0-7364-2346-X

www.randomhouse.com/kids/disney

Printed in the United States of America

13 12 11 10 9 8 7 6   First Edition

DISNEP · PIXAR

Cars

Faster Than Fast

As told by Doc Hudson to Irene Trimble

Illustrated by Carson Van Osten
Designed by Tony Fejeran of Disney Publishing's Global Design Group
Inspired by the art and character designs created by Pixar Animation Studios

A Special Introduction by
Lightning McQueen!

KA-CHOW!

Ya know, when I first drove (okay, okay, CRASHED) into Radiator Springs and met the judge, Doc Hudson, I thought he was nothing but a grumpy old grandpa car. And it was pretty obvious he didn't like me all that much, either. He thought I was just another cocky race car, and he sure let me know it. I was real angry at first. I mean, he didn't even know I was famous. But in the end, I suppose he was right. That old guy really did teach me a lot.

For one thing, I learned about friendship. Okay, okay, it's true: Lightning McQueen here didn't have too many cars to call friends before he met Doc and the folks of Radiator Springs. And ya know, Doc even knew a thing or two about racing! He taught me a move that I used in the Piston Cup Championship race. You'll hear more about that later, since I don't want to ruin Doc's book for you, but by the end of the race, I had learned something even more important: sometimes it's good to slow down and enjoy the drive.

I was honored when Doc asked me to write the introduction for this book of his. If I were you, I'd read it. Old Doc is my crew chief now, and he's the best one around. If you listen to him, you might also learn a thing or two.

Well, it's back to my training schedule. So turn the page, read what Doc has to say, and for now . . . *Ka-chow!*

—Lightning McQueen

Chapter 1

My name's Doc Hudson. Folks round here say that every car has a story. I don't know if that's so, but I can tell you this: I've got one heck of a story for you! Oh, I know that you may not believe that one car could get itself into a world of trouble and turn a whole town on its ear. But I'm here to tell you how one car did!

For me, it all started when I woke up one morning and found our little town of Radiator Springs ripped to shreds.

But the worst part was the road. It was completely torn up!

Sheriff came over to give me the scoop on the previous night's events. He said that some hot-rodder had passed our little Radiator Springs billboard (Sheriff's favorite napping spot) going way over the speed limit.

Course, Sheriff can't go any faster than forty-five miles per hour these days without letting out a little backfire. But he wasn't about to let a "crazy hot-rodder" get away (and that's an exact quote). For the first time in years, Sheriff even turned on his flashing red lights.

Then he started up that cranky old engine of his and took off after the hot rod with a blast of backfire you could hear all the way to the Interstate!

Suddenly, the hot rod started zig-zagging all over the road. We figured out later that every time he'd heard Sheriff's backfire, he'd thought he was being shot at—so he'd driven even faster. Sheriff said that by the time the car sped through the heart of our little town, he must've been doing 120 miles per hour!

No one in Radiator Springs saw it coming. I was locked in my office for the night and didn't hear a thing. Lizzie was snoozing away on her porch. (We all know how much Lizzie loves naps. I love 'em, too! She may be the oldest resident in

town, but I'm not too far behind her.)
And Red was watering his flower garden.
That fire truck sure takes pride in that
garden of his.

And Fillmore . . . heck, he was doing
what he does every night—just passing
the time staring at Radiator Springs' only
traffic light.

Yup, that old hippie Fillmore was
trying to convince his neighbor Sarge that
the timing of the traffic blinks was off.

"I'm telling you, man! Every third blink
is slower," Fillmore insisted as he stared at
the light.

All in all, it was a typical night's entertainment in Radiator Springs. Of course, that all changed shortly thereafter. Sheriff went racing down Main Street in hot pursuit of the criminal. And since folks had seen hardly a single car pass through town since they'd built the Interstate, it was pretty darned exciting.

Everybody in town but me was out by then, and they all cringed as they saw the flashy car heading for Sally's motel at lightning speed. Sheriff gave the car some credit: he did his best to swerve around the small huts that served as guest rooms. But then he got turned around and ran into the barbed wire fencing. The stranger managed to drag the fence all the way through town without slowing down at all, it seemed.

Sheriff yelled for everyone to take cover as the out-of-control car plowed through a row of oilcans in front of Flo's V8 Café and headed toward Luigi's Casa

Della Tires. Luigi and Guido had just
finished stacking their 98% OFF snow
tire display. Somehow the fast-wheeling
stranger was drawn to the stack of tires
like a bee to honey and smacked into it
head-on, causing tires to fly, flip, and roll
all over the place. Guido remarkably and
nimbly caught each one.

But that car wasn't finished turning
Radiator Springs on its ear yet. No, he
dragged the fence through Red's flower

garden and wrapped it around the statue of Radiator Springs' founding father, Stanley! Then the hot rod really panicked. His reaction was simply to gun it, hauling Stanley behind him like a water-skier! Together, the old car statue and the newcomer tore holes in the road the size of boulders as they bounced and scraped down Main Street.

The car finally wrapped the fence around some telephone wires and catapulted that statue right back onto its pedestal in front of the courthouse. Lizzie couldn't believe her eyes when she saw the statue flying through the air, and

Fillmore was sure he'd imagined the whole
darn thing! Sheriff knew it was real enough
as the hot-rodder stared helplessly at him,
finally stuck at a standstill, suspended from
the telephone wires.

My buddy Sheriff marched right up to
the kid and said, "Boy, you're in a heap of
trouble." Then that hot rod passed out,
and Sheriff called Mater the tow truck to
tow him off to the impound for the night.

Chapter 2

Well, once Sheriff finished telling me the story, I knew it was time for me to change my flaps and be *Judge* Hudson instead of *Doc* Hudson. The folks of Radiator Springs were in a real tizzy, all right. Angrier than an 18-wheeler with a string of flat tires. And, being the only judge in town, I was the one who was going to put the car who had made them angry in jail for a long, long time.

So I got ready and waited in my office to be called out to meet the accused. The problem was, Sheriff couldn't get the townsfolk to stop yelling at the stranger long enough for him to call the court to order.

"Hey, you scratched my paint!" shouted Ramone, the town's lowrider. He owned Ramone's House of Body Art. I could still remember when his shop was busy from dawn till dusk every day of the week. But with local business being as bad as it had, he'd been passing the days painting himself. He was one smart-looking car, all right.

Lizzie was stunned by what had happened to Stanley's statue, and she was shouting about it for all the town to hear.

"Hey!" Sheriff finally shouted, trying to quiet the little room. "Anyone want to be his lawyer?"

Of course nobody did—no one, that is, except Mater. We all knew Mater well enough to know he just wanted to be the stranger's friend.

"Shoot, I'll do it, Sheriff!" he said.

Then Sheriff called the court to order and announced my entrance (one of the few perks of being a judge). Of course, I entered madder than could be—especially since I had heard Sheriff's story about what the hotshot car had done the night before.

"All right," I said, wanting to get a good look at this stranger. "I wanna know who's responsible for wrecking my town, Sheriff. I want his hood on a platter. I'm gonna put him in jail till he rots. No— check that. I'm gonna put him in jail till the jail rots on top of him, and then I'm gonna move him to a new jail and let that jail rot. I'm—"

I stopped short. I have to say that I was not expecting to see what was before my eyes when I finally reached the top of my podium. I saw one thing and one thing only: a race car. A rookie race car with a heap of attitude and pride.

I wanted nothing to do with him. Had I seen him the night before or known who

he was, I never even would have had a trial. I would have called the whole thing off and let him race away into the sunset or whatever those fancy new race cars do. Race cars. I'm telling you, they're no good.

"Throw him out of here, Sheriff," I said, angrier than ever. "I want him out of our town! Case dismissed."

Well, I can't tell you that the townsfolk were very happy about my decision, but I knew what I was doing.

That kid was going to do nothing but cause more trouble. Professional racing for cars is a nasty business, and the race cars are just as nasty. And I should know. Aw, heck, I'm getting sidetracked. You'll just have to wait for that part of the story. But I DO know more about the racing business than anybody else around, including that hotshot red racer, who we learned was named Lightning McQueen.

Of course, as soon as I made my decision, Sally arrived in the courtroom. Sally's a pretty blue sports car who runs the Cozy Cone Motel and also serves as the town's lawyer. That McQueen fell for her good looks right away and even asked her out. Little did he know that she was ready to get down to business—the business of making him pay for all the damage he had done.

"What do you want, Sally?" I asked as she approached me. I knew she was going to try to keep that car in town—you know, to fix things up. Well, I wanted nothing to do with it.

"Come on!" she said, filled with as much anger toward the stranger as the rest of us were. "Make this guy fix the road. The town needs this."

I refused. Big mistake.

Sally turned to the townsfolk. "Fellow citizens, you're all aware of our town's proud history. Radiator Springs. The glorious jewel strung on the necklace of Highway Sixty-six," she began. "It is our job and our pleasure to take care of the travelers on our stretch of that road." Sally was determined.

"But how, I ask you, are we to care for those travelers if there is no road for them to drive on?" When she asked Flo

how she expected to sell gas at her café if there was no road for folks to get to her, Flo realized she might have to close up and leave town. And if Flo left and there was no gas, how would the folks of Radiator Springs survive?

"Fix the road!" all the townsfolk roared at McQueen.

"Seems like my mind has been changed for me," I muttered.

And so the flashy race car began his sentence in Radiator Springs and was not allowed to leave till he fixed the road.

Chapter 3

Well, not to say "I told you so," but I did. That race car was nothing but trouble, just as I had predicted. He was hoping to take Sally out to dinner on his way out of town and ended up instead with Bessie, the finest road-paving machine ever built. That didn't set too well with that fancy red race car, as you might imagine.

The proud kid got even madder when he saw how much of Main Street he had to pave with dear Bessie. "'Bout five days' worth of hard labor," I told him.

"You gotta be kidding me," that spoiled kid howled. "FIVE DAYS?"

Sure enough, the first chance he got, he made a run for it, yelling, "California, here I come!" Till he sputtered and pooped out, that is. I'll bet you can guess why that race car stopped dead in the middle of the street right at the edge of town.

"No, no, no, no!" he shouted, coming to a complete stop. "Out of gas? How can I be out of gas?"

Just then, Sheriff and Sally came out from behind the WELCOME TO RADIATOR SPRINGS sign, giggling at the hotshot as he gasped in disbelief. McQueen hadn't counted on Sheriff taking out most of his gas while he was asleep in the impound. We weren't as dumb as that boy thought we were.

At that point, the rookie realized he had no choice. For the first time in his cushy life, he had to work. And so, later that afternoon, the whole town watched as McQueen slowly did some real, hard labor, hauling poor Bessie under a blazing sun.

The townsfolk were very entertained by the whole situation. Sheriff joined Fillmore and Sarge at Flo's V8 Café for a quart of oil as they all watched the rookie at work. As for old Lizzie, she didn't mind gazing at that young fella flexing his fenders in the sun.

"Down in front," she shouted to Red. "Some of us want to get a look!"

I think it was just then that Bessie belched a wad of tar, which landed right on the rookie's lightning-bolt sticker. It was almost more than that proud hotshot could take.

"I shouldn't have to put up with this!" he yelled. "I am a precisional instrument of speed and aerodynamics!"

Nobody but Mater was much impressed, and Mater was only interested because he didn't understand what that hotshot had said.

"I'm a very famous race car!" the rookie yelled angrily.

That was when Luigi perked up. As the town's tire expert, he loved racing, and he couldn't help being excited. "You are a famous race car?" he asked. "A real race car?" Luigi was in the middle of a dream come true. "I have followed racing my entire life! My whole life!"

"Then you know who I am," the rookie said. "I'm Lightning McQueen." You would have thought he'd invented a cure for rust the way he announced his name. Unfortunately for him, nobody cared much. Even Luigi lost interest when he learned that McQueen was in the Piston Cup circuit. (Luigi only followed Italian racing.)

To top it off, McQueen heard an old radio blaring into the street from Lizzie's front porch. It was tuned to an interview with Chick Hicks, McQueen's rival for the Piston Cup and for the admiring eyes of a big company named Dinoco. You have to understand that for McQueen life was all about racing, and he was trying to get to a racetrack in California to become a superstar and win a tiebreaker race. The winner would get none other than the Piston Cup—the prize trophy of the racing season. And Chick was already practicing on the track and getting all the attention that was supposed to be McQueen's.

Chick was also getting the attention of Dinoco, and both of them wanted Dinoco as a new sponsor. The Dinoco car could get lots of money and lots of fans.

And so that was when McQueen started rushing to finish the job. He pushed Bessie a lot harder than he should have. Boy, was he struggling! And in one hour? Well, let's just say that the town found the biggest mess anyone had ever seen. Every pothole and chunk of asphalt was covered with ugly globs of tar.

"I'm done!" McQueen announced, as if he could possibly convince us that the road was in the shape it had been in when he had first driven into town.

When Sally told him it looked awful, McQueen smirked and said, "Now it matches the rest of the town!"

Yup, that one hurt. Red burst into tears. (Boy, a fire truck can come up with a lot of water when he cries!) Everybody else was just plain shocked.

Now, *right's right* is what I always say, and there was no way this was right. "The deal was you fix the road, not make it worse," I told McQueen. "Now scrape it off and start over again!"

McQueen said, "Hey, look, grandpa, I'm not a bulldozer. I'm a race car!"

I had had enough from the young hotshot.

"Race me," I said to McQueen. "If you win, you go and I fix the road. If I win, you do the road MY way!"

Chapter 4

Now, I know that McQueen thought it was a joke. He was happy to take that challenge. Thought it was a fast ticket out of town. To be honest with you, I think everyone else in Radiator Springs thought the same thing. They were afraid, too— afraid that our section of old Highway 66 would never be fixed now. But the town turned out at Willys Butte for the race anyway. Guess they hadn't had that much excitement in years. They all lined up on the cliff as McQueen and I took to the starting line.

Luigi told McQueen that it had always been Guido's dream to give a pit stop to a real race car and offered Guido's help. But that hotshot rookie thought no one in this town was good enough to change his tires.

"The race is only one lap, guys. Uno

lapo," he said, making fun of Guido for not speaking English. "I work so-lo me-o."

Sheriff read the rules, then gave us the go-ahead to start our engines. Everyone sure looked worried when they heard mine next to McQueen's. Gotta admit I sounded like a windup toy next to a jet plane.

When Luigi gave us the flag, McQueen took off down the dirt road in a plume of dust. The crowd cheered until the dust cleared and they saw I was still on the starting line. Hadn't moved an inch.

I called Mater over. The rusty tow truck stayed beside me as we slowly drove down the track, far behind McQueen.

"Might need a little help," I said to Mater as we chugged along. "You got your tow cable?"

"I always got my tow cable," Mater told me. "Why?"

"Ohhhh, just in case," I said as I watched McQueen head for the second turn on the dirt road. Now, I'm betting you're thinking you know where this story is headed: old car versus flashy race car, and the old car conks out, right? Wrong! I knew exactly what I was doing. Sure enough, McQueen lost control and dropped off a low cliff exactly where I thought he would—landed in a ditch filled with cacti. He was stucker than stuck.

"You race like you fix roads!" I called down to him. "Lousy!"

McQueen tried revving his engine, but it was no use. "Have fun fishing!" I told Mater as he dropped his towline to McQueen.

It wasn't long before the rookie was

working on our road again. Folks felt a little sorry for him, getting beat so bad *and* working in the hot sun all day.

Fillmore offered him some of his homemade organic fuel. Ramone even offered to do a paint job on the cactus scratches. But McQueen wasn't interested. He just kept scraping that tar off the road, mumbling, "'You race like you fix roads.' I'll show him!"

Okay, I gotta admit that the kid had spunk. I never saw anyone work so hard on anything. By the time the sun set, McQueen was repaving that busted road

with sputtering Bessie. And this time, he was doing it right.

That rookie's complaining all night was music to my ears. But the next morning, the darndest thing happened. Everyone woke to the sound of Mater yelling, "Whee-hee!"

I looked out my office window and saw that goofy tow truck twirling around on the most beautifully paved stretch of road I'd ever seen!

Flo got out there with Ramone and they were cruising it low and slow.

"It's like it was-a paved by angels!" Luigi shouted. The whole town was delighted. That stretch of shiny new blacktop sure did brighten up the place. Made folks remember what it felt like when Highway 66 was in its prime.

I went looking for McQueen but found only Bessie parked off by herself. I found the kid out at the butte. The rookie was still determined to make that turn he'd blown in our race. Practiced it over and over. Kept blowing it over and over, too. But he wouldn't give up, I can tell you that. He gave it all he had with every try. I think that was the first time the kid got to me.

That day, I tried to give him some advice on how to race on dirt. Told him to turn right to go left. McQueen thought he was the only race car in town, but what he didn't realize—well, as I said, I'm getting ahead of myself. The point is, he wasn't about to take advice from an old-timer like me.

I had to laugh, though, when I turned away and pretended not to be looking. McQueen tried the turn just as I had told him to. Of course, he did it all wrong and ended up back in the ditch. I guessed he was just gonna have to learn things his own way—with a mouthful of cactus needles.

Chapter 5

There was still plenty of road left for McQueen to fix, and since he was staying in town, the folks of Radiator Springs were hoping that the rookie might come and visit their shops. After all, nobody had seen a customer in quite some time.

Course, McQueen wasn't interested in Lizzie's old Highway 66 memorabilia shop. McQueen wanted to get out of this town, not buy souvenirs to remember it. Turned his nose up at Fillmore's organic fuel again, too.

Luigi noticed that McQueen's tires were looking a little worn. "You make-a such a nice road," Luigi told the rookie. "Luigi take-a good care of you!"

He and Guido offered McQueen a
good deal on a set of tires, but McQueen
wasn't much interested in helping out the
local economy. He was still in a big hurry
to get the work done and go, still dreaming
about that big race in California in a couple
of days.

"Look," McQueen finally told Luigi,
giving him the brush-off, "I get all my tires
for free." He acted as if he owned the
whole world and we were just a bunch of
dumb country bumpkins.

But that didn't stop the folks of
Radiator Springs from being nice. Sally
even offered to let McQueen stay at her
motel instead of the impound.

And of course, nobody was as ready to be friendly as Mater was. Mater even took McQueen out tractor tipping. He showed McQueen that if you beeped your horn at a farm tractor real sudden, the sleepy machine would fall right over.

Mater loved tipping tractors. McQueen wasn't really excited by the whole thing, especially since he didn't have a horn. (Some of those new race cars—I swear they don't think they need anything, not even real headlights. Instead they have stickers for headlights.) Still, McQueen tried to join Mater. He revved his engine as loud as he could, and soon a whole bunch of tractors moaned, tipped over, and backfired. That was when Frank the

combine arrived, and Mater and McQueen took off as fast as they could. Frank was one mean machine when it came to protecting his tractors.

McQueen and Mater returned to town, giggling and joking. Sally watched the whole thing from her window at her motel. She saw a stunned McQueen watch Mater drive backward all over the place. (That's another thing these new race cars don't have—rearview mirrors!) Sally overheard McQueen tell Mater his dreams of being a great big star, winning all the races, riding in helicopters—the whole works. Mater was delighted. He even asked McQueen if he'd let him have a helicopter ride someday when McQueen was a big champion.

"Yeah, yeah, yeah, yeah. Sure," McQueen promised, not really expecting to have to make good on the promise.

Then the strangest thing happened. As Mater turned to leave, he told McQueen, "I knowed it. I knowed I made a good choice."

"In what?" asked the rookie.

"My best friend," Mater said with a great big smile. "See you tomorrow, buddy."

For the first time in a while, I think the rookie didn't have anything to say. His jaw dropped. You see, he had never had any real friends. Lots of fans and reporters and whatnot . . . but no friends.

Meanwhile, Sally doubted that McQueen really meant the promise he had made to Mater about a helicopter ride. But she sure knew that Mater trusted McQueen. She worried that that young hot rod would never come back to Radiator Springs once

he hit the fast lane again. She was afraid Mater was going to get his feelings hurt real bad.

When Sally saw Mater zipping down the road in reverse, singing about having a new friend, she knew she'd have to have a talk with McQueen. As soon as McQueen got to his motel room, she drove right up to him.

"Hey, Stickers!" she called out. "Did you mean it?"

"What?" asked McQueen.

"That you'll get him a ride?" Sally said, referring to McQueen's promise to Mater.

"Oh, who knows?" the rookie hotshot replied. "I mean, first things first. I gotta get outta here and make the race."

Sally frowned. "Uh-huh," she said. "You know, Mater trusts you." She wanted McQueen to know that a promise was a promise. And she expected him to keep his promise to Mater.

Chapter 6

The next morning, things got worse. The hotshot came into my office while I was busy with a patient. Of all the cars in town, that patient just happened to be Sheriff. He had come in for a smog check, and as we all know, that's pretty private business.

"Get a good peek, city boy?" Sheriff said to McQueen from up on the lift. McQueen backed out of my office, a little embarrassed.

That was when the kid wandered into my garage, and what did he find? Three Piston Cup trophies with my name on them. (I told you I knew a bit about racing myself. But nobody else in town knew I had been a race car, and I had decided long before that I wasn't going to tell them, either.)

McQueen was shocked. He started

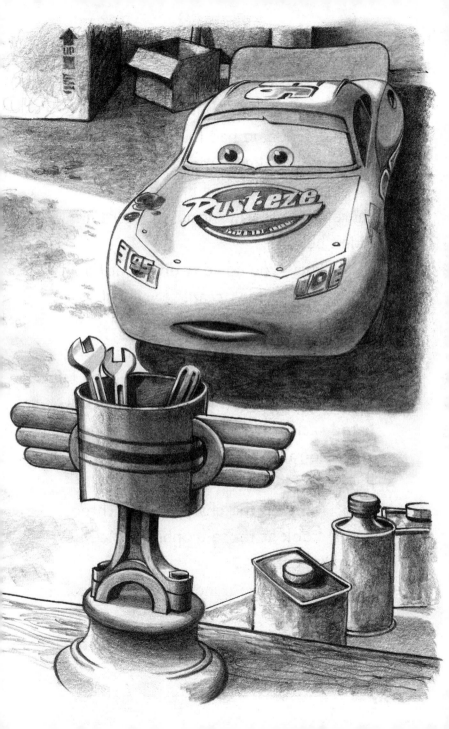

digging through my things. There were signs all over that garage. NO TRESSPASSING, PRIVATE PROPERTY! But that didn't stop the kid. Once he had found those trophies, he wanted to know more.

I remember going in and finding him there staring away, snooping where he didn't belong.

"I knew you couldn't drive, but I didn't know you couldn't read!" I yelled. I was mad—madder than I'd been the day when, at the top of my racing career, I'd gotten into a wreck and had practically been left for junkyard parts. Now, that was why I hated racing, and that was why I knew that a rookie race car would do little good for my small town.

"You won the championship three times! Look at those trophies!" McQueen said, all excited.

"All I see is a bunch of empty cups," I grumbled.

That was all that those trophies meant

to me. I knew that McQueen wasn't ready to understand that some things are more important than trophies and rich sponsors that give you helicopter rides. Things like knowing who your friends are and how to treat 'em.

But that wasn't the worst of it. McQueen left my garage and told everyone in town who I was. He rushed out onto that new road and went to Flo's café, yelling, "Oh, my gosh! Guys! Did you know Doc is a famous race car? He's a real racing legend!"

Luckily, no one in town believed McQueen's story. They thought the heat was finally gettin' to him!

"Dude's hallucinating, man!" Fillmore said about the wild-eyed rookie.

But McQueen told anyone who'd listen, "He won three Piston Cups!"

"He did what in his cup?" Mater asked him.

McQueen didn't stop to think that if no one in town knew my story, maybe I didn't want 'em to. Guess that's part of being a rookie: you gotta learn when to stop and think.

Later that day, Sally took McQueen for a ride. (I think she was starting to like the guy.) Meanwhile, some tractors had escaped from the nearby corral. So while the town was busy wrangling them, I took the opportunity to slip on my old racing tires, and I secretly headed to the butte. I had that old track all to myself.

I just wanted to see if this old engine could still open up and take the road like it used to, feel the wind rush by one more time. And what d'ya know? I still had it! I

raced up and down like I was a kid myself!

What I didn't know was that the rookie was out there, too, watching me. Apparently, he was out there looking for a lost tractor. Guess he saw me take that turn he kept blowing. It gave my advice on turning on dirt a whole new glow.

He came rushing over to me, yelling, "Doc! Wow! Your driving is incredible!"

"Wonderful," I told him. "Now go away."

But McQueen wouldn't accept that.

He said, "C'mon, I'm a race car. You're a much older race car, but under the hood you and I are the same."

No way were we the same. I told

McQueen my story—about how I'd figured out that I was only as good as my last win on the racing circuit. I even told him about my big crash—the one that ended my career.

The crowds loved me for being a great race car. But when I crashed, they just moved on to the next young rookie and forgot all about me. Lucky I found my way to Radiator Springs is all I can say. McQueen had never given much thought

The Daily Exhaust   **FINAL**

CRASH!

Season Ender Fender Bender Puts Young Hornet In Garage

to anything like that. Fact is, I'd kept all that a secret for so long I couldn't even remember the last time I'd talked about it. It did remind me of the days when I was one of the greats, though.

I told McQueen that we weren't the same—not in the ways that really counted. "When was the last time you cared about something except yourself, hot rod? You name me one time?" I asked him.

Like I thought, McQueen couldn't come up with a thing, and I could tell it bothered him. The rookie didn't like my saying that these were good folks around

here who cared about one another and I
didn't want them depending on someone
they couldn't count on!

But McQueen gave me, Doc Hudson,
a bit of my own medicine that day. "You've
been here how long?" McQueen asked
me. "And your friends don't even know
who you are! Who's caring only about
himself?"

We both acted mad, and I told
McQueen to finish the job and get out of
town! But the truth is, we gave each other
a lot to think about.

Chapter 7

Well, the very next morning, the road was finished. And McQueen was gone.

"He's done!" Mater said softly. "He musta' finished while we were all sleeping!"

"Good riddance," I thought. But when I looked at that long stretch of new blacktop, I had to smile.

That road turned out pretty darn good, slick as a whistle! Had great traction, too. It almost looked like Highway 66 in its heyday.

Everyone came out to see the finished road. They couldn't wait to tell McQueen what a good job he'd done. They stared off down that road for a long time lookin' for him, but McQueen was nowhere in sight.

"He's gone?" Flo asked. There was barely a dry eye in Radiator Springs that morning. Red burst into tears and drove right through Luigi's latest tower of tires.

"Well," Sheriff said, "we wouldn't want him to miss that race of his." You won't believe this, but I think I caught Sheriff sniffling.

"What's wrong with Red?" someone finally asked.

Everyone turned—and saw that it was McQueen who'd asked the question.

"Lightning!" everyone shouted. "There you are!" Yup. Folks had grown to like the kid.

Everyone was excited, all right, but nobody was more pleased than old Mater. "Aw, I knew you wouldn't leave without

saying goodbye!" he said to the rookie, giving him a friendly slug. (That's Mater's version of a hug, you know.)

Me, I couldn't figure out why the rookie hadn't just blown out of town for good. McQueen told everyone he couldn't leave yet.

"I'm not sure these tires can get me all the way to California," he said, grinning.

"Pit stop?" Guido asked, filled with excitement.

"Yeah," said McQueen. "Anybody know what time Luigi's opens?"

Luigi was stunned. He thanked the stars as they rolled McQueen into Luigi's Casa Della Tires. "I am filled with-a tears of ecstasy, for this is the most glorious day of my life!" Luigi gushed as he outfitted McQueen with four brand-new whitewall tires.

"Pit stop!" Guido shouted, overjoyed that he could pretend to do a pit stop by changing tires for McQueen. The little guy headed over to McQueen with a hydraulic lug wrench. Then he got to work!

McQueen checked out his new look in Luigi's three-way mirror. Those tires might not have been what you usually see on the race car circuit, but they looked good on the rookie, and they sure made Luigi and Guido happy.

Next, McQueen headed to Fillmore's Organic Fuel. The sign said TASTE-IN, so the rookie rolled right in.

Under the tie-dyed banner in
Fillmore's garden, McQueen filled up on
some of his 100 percent organic fuel.
"Wow!" McQueen said to old Fillmore.
"This stuff is great! Why haven't I heard of
it before?"

Fillmore explained his government
conspiracy theory as McQueen bought
himself a full case; then the kid headed
over to Sarge's supply shop.

"Would you look at that!" Flo said as
every business in town flipped its sign
from CLOSED to OPEN. "We finally got
ourselves a customer." McQueen was the
first customer in Radiator Springs in a long

time, and folks were mighty excited.

McQueen picked out some night-vision goggles at Sarge's. Then he even went to old Lizzie's souvenir shop for some bumper stickers!

At the end of the day, the rookie finally stopped at Ramone's for a whole new paint job. Everyone was lined up outside the paint shop as Sally came around the corner.

Sally stopped just as Mater said, "Ladies and gentlecars, please welcome the new LIGHTNING MCQUEEN!"

Sally was pretty surprised to see McQueen roll out all glistening and fresh from his makeover. Ramone had detailed him to perfection, even airbrushed him a new lightning bolt.

From McQueen's whitewall tires to the Radiator Springs bumper stickers all over the rookie's fender, Sally could see that he had shopped at every store in town.

"What do you think?" he asked her with a wink. "Radiator Springs looks pretty good on me!"

"It looks like you helped everyone in town!" Sally said, beaming at him.

McQueen had one more surprise. He looked at old Lizzie and gave her a signal. Lizzie seemed to forget for a second what she was supposed to do, then suddenly remembered. She gave her old radio a kick, and the streets of Radiator Springs filled with music.

Then, out of nowhere, the purple neon sign over Ramone's paint shop flickered to life; then the red one over Luigi's tire shop began to gleam, and the pink one over Flo's V8 Café started to shine! One by one, every neon sign in town came back to life. Old Main Street, Highway 66, glowed in a light and warmth that was truly beautiful!

You see, when the town had seen that bit of new road, all beautiful and smooth, they had decided that their shops needed a little fixing up, too. They had painted, cleaned, and even helped McQueen surprise Sally with the fixed-up neon. Sally had always wanted to see the town back in its former glory, and now it was.

That night, all the cars in town cruised the old highway just like they had in the old days—listening to music and loving the road.

I tell you, it was a night to remember. Ramone and Flo, Red and Lizzie, even Sarge and Fillmore were cruising side by side. McQueen kept trying to cruise with Sally, but each time, someone else seemed to get in the way.

It was about then that we noticed all the headlights coming down the road. Everyone thought the neon lights of Radiator Springs were drawin' cars in to take a look!

"Customers!" Flo shouted as those lights got closer to town.

But I'm afraid that wasn't what they turned out to be.

Chapter 8

A helicopter light swept over Radiator Springs. "We have found McQueen!" a voice blared over Main Street. Suddenly, an army of reporters rushed into town.

They swarmed McQueen like bees, shouting his name and pushing everyone else, including Sally, out of the way. They pulled Mater aside and asked him if McQueen was his prisoner. They asked McQueen if he'd had a nervous breakdown.

When they got a look at his whitewall tires, they asked if he was going bald! I tell you, those reporters were crazy to make a story out of anything.

McQueen kept calling out to Sally, but the press pushed her farther and farther away. The folks here in Radiator Springs just didn't know what had hit 'em. Mostly, everyone ducked for cover.

Then Mack, the huge semitrailer who

was supposed to carry McQueen to California, rolled into town. I think that old rig had been McQueen's only friend (before he'd arrived at our town, that is), 'cause those two seemed mighty happy to see each other. I tell you, that big truck was in tears when he laid eyes on McQueen.

"Thank the manufacturer you're alive!" he called out to the kid.

Above all the commotion and flashing cameras, McQueen's agent started talkin' over Mack's speakerphone. This guy, Harv, told McQueen he'd better hightail it to

California pronto. Harv said that if he didn't, he could kiss his fame and fortune from Dinoco—not to mention winning the Piston Cup—goodbye.

I could tell that the kid was really torn. He scanned the crowd for Sally while his agent kept telling him to get in that truck. Yup, he was gonna have to make a tough choice and say goodbye to somebody right then and there.

By the time the rookie made it over to Sally, there really wasn't much he could say. But I don't think he'd ever felt so bad about anything in his whole life. And with that, McQueen backed into Mack's trailer.

"I didn't get to say goodbye to him," Mater said to me sadly.

Just then, a reporter called out to me, "Hey, are you Doc Hudson?"

When I told her I was, she yelled back, "Thanks for the call!"

Sally heard what that reporter said. Boy, was I in trouble then. It didn't take her a second to figure out I was the one who had told the press McQueen was here. She let me know that I, and not anyone else, was being selfish. She was right. I guess I thought I was doing the town a favor by turning in McQueen. But I was wrong. I did it because . . . well, because I was bitter about the whole racing scene and I didn't want that kid ruining what I had in my town. I hadn't given a thought to what the rookie had done for our town or what he had learned about from us—friendship and promises, and the good stuff in life.

When the doors on Mack's trailer swung shut, part of the heart of folks in Radiator Springs closed, too. We all watched that crowd of reporters follow Mack as he headed to the Interstate, toward the race in California. And just like that, everyone was gone.

I watched the folks of Radiator Springs drive home that night. One by one, they sadly turned off their neon lights. It was then that I saw how much hurt I had caused just tryin' to protect myself.

That was when I figured out what I had to do to make it right. Course, I knew I needed a little help from my friends to make it happen.

A couple of days later, Lizzie rolled a banged-up TV to Flo's. Somehow, that old gal managed to tune it to the Piston Cup live! Red helped her, and soon Sally showed up. They all gathered around that little TV and listened as the announcer called it the race of the century.

"And there he is," the announcer said, "Lightning McQueen!"

Out on the track, next to the kid, was Chick Hicks. Chick had grown mighty used to being in the spotlight since McQueen had disappeared in Radiator Springs. Planned on keeping it that way, too. As far as he was concerned, the race was his.

But next to Chick was the crowd's sentimental favorite, The King himself, Strip Weathers. After a long and great career, this would be the final race for The King, and everyone wished him the best.

The crowd was on their back wheels when the starter dropped the green flag. Chick and The King blasted off the starting line, but McQueen idled for a second. That was long enough to put Chick and The King well ahead of the kid.

By the time they reached the fiftieth lap, McQueen had caught up to the leaders. All three cars were in a dead heat, battling for first place, but it seemed McQueen's mind wasn't even in the race. Suddenly, he veered too close to the wall, and before he knew it, the rookie spun himself right off the track and into the infield.

The crowd gasped. McQueen just idled there in the infield, watching Chick and The King zoom away. I could tell the kid's heart just wasn't in it. My bet was that his heart was still with the pretty blue sports car he'd left behind in Radiator Springs.

"Kid, are you okay?" Mack asked over his headset. Then Mack handed the headset to me. Yeah, I was there, all right. What did you expect? I wasn't going to let down a friend!

"I didn't come all this way to see you quit!" I yelled to McQueen.

I knew that the kid was surprised. Bet he was even more surprised when he looked at pit row and saw Flo, Ramone, Sarge, Fillmore, and Mater! Yup, it was Team McQueen, ready and waiting. Even Guido and Luigi were there, overjoyed finally to be part of a real pit crew!

I gotta say, it felt pretty good when the crowd noticed who McQueen's crew chief was. See, Ramone did me up in the same gleaming blue I wore when I was the Fabulous Hudson Hornet. The whole stadium recognized me. They cheered just like they had when I was on top. And here

I'd thought they'd all forgotten. But enough about me. We had to get that kid back in the race!

"All right," I said to McQueen, "if you can drive as good as you can fix a road, then you can win this with your eyes shut!"

I know they were cheering in Radiator Springs when McQueen tore back onto that track like he owned it! The rookie had lost a lap and needed to catch up.

Chick took a swipe at the kid. Rammed him hard, spinning him into a 180. But McQueen passed him anyway, even running a stretch in reverse, which sure made Mater proud.

The boys from Casa Della Tires put every other pit crew to shame that day, too. Luigi and Guido changed out McQueen's tires in record time during the next pit stop. The kid was back on the track before both challengers.

It was down to the last lap. "This is it!" I told McQueen. "You only got two turns left!"

McQueen took the first turn high and close to the wall. Chick saw him make his move and rammed McQueen again. This time, the kid spun off the track. "McQueen's out of the race!" the announcer called to the stunned crowd.

But no one knew that the kid had learned a trick from an old-timer. Turn right to go left was what he did! Spun himself right back onto the track and into the lead!

The crowd was cheering. There was nothing between McQueen and the finish line now.

Chick gunned it. He knew he couldn't catch McQueen, but he wasn't about to come in after The King. . . .

And *bam!* Just like that, Chick rammed The King into the wall and sped off after McQueen. The crowd was shocked. Heartbroken was more like it. They watched The King crash and roll to a stop. The old guy would finish his career without crossing the finish line. I can't tell you what kind of memories that brought back for me.

Now, I've seen a lot of things in my time, but I'd never seen anything like this. A foot from the finish line, McQueen

looked up at the stadium's big screen and
stopped! He saw The King and realized
that the legend was in trouble. Before I
knew it, McQueen started rolling in
reverse. While that nasty Chick crossed
the finish line, McQueen pulled up behind
The King!

The rest of the crew was confused,
but I knew exactly what the rookie was
doing. And I have to tell you, I was mighty
proud as I listened over my headset.

"You just gave up the Piston Cup, you
know that?" The King said to McQueen.

"Ah, this grumpy old race car I know

once told me something: it's just an empty cup," McQueen answered as he pushed The King toward the finish line.

Well, Chick won the cup that day, but nobody much noticed. It was McQueen who won their hearts. He even got offered the big Dinoco sponsorship! But he turned it down. Go figure! He was going to stick with his old sponsor, which had given him his first big break.

Although McQueen kept racing, he left the fast life behind. He made his headquarters right here in Radiator Springs and made me his crew chief.

Of course, the town isn't the same anymore, visitors poking all over the place. Seems McQueen told every car on the racing circuit about Radiator Springs. Between the shoppers and the visitors of the new racing museum, the folks around here barely have a minute to themselves. But there it is: we're still all here and making a living in our happy home.

Speaking of the museum, they went and built a wing named after me. Can you believe that? Now I gotta keep those trophies all shined up—that is, when I'm not out racing McQueen on dirt. We're working on breaking a tie these days. Ha!

And that's the story of how one flashy race car nearly ruined our town . . . and became part of our family instead. And if you don't believe me, ask my new racing buddy yourself.